Incessantly Bigfooting
Light-Hearted Stories from a Lifelong Bigfoot Enthusiast

Kevin Llewellyn

Copyright © 2022 Kevin Llewellyn

All rights reserved. No part of this book may be reproduced or transmitted in any form or by any means, electronic or mechanical, including photocopying, recording or by any information storage and retrieval system without permission in writing from the publisher.

Rusty Truck Publishing—Spokane, WA
ISBN: 979-8-9856917-0-2
Library of Congress Control Number: 2022902630
Title: Incessantly Bigfooting: Light-Hearted Stories from a Lifelong Bigfoot Enthusiast
Author: Kevin Llewellyn
Digital distribution | 2022
Paperback | 2022

This is a work of fiction. The characters, names, incidents, places, and dialogue are products of the author's imagination, and are not to be construed as real.

Dedication

This book is dedicated to my dad who spent many hours with me in the forest and on the water. He taught me to enjoy the magnificence of nature and respect it. This is also dedicated to my wife, Carol. I cherish her support and interest in my pursuits (and the great homemade cookies and snacks she has for me when I return home from a long camping trip!)

Table of Contents

Introduction

I was fortunate at ten years of age to see Roger Patterson present in person the Patterson-Gimlin film at the Spokane Coliseum in Spokane, Washington. I got his autograph that night. Later, I became a member of his Northwest Research Association and received bulletins/newsletters that he wrote. These rare items of Bigfoot history will be mentioned throughout the book.

Through the decades, I have had many encounters and experiences that I can only attribute to Bigfoot activity. I do question everything I hear and see. Every investigator has their own approach. My approach is to have respect for the forest and Bigfoot. I try many things to both make Bigfoot curious about me and feel comfortable to approach. Over the years, I have a list of things I do and have had good luck. Whatever works for you, keep doing it.

This book contains true stories that actually happened over the decades of some of my

Bigfoot experiences and sighting. There are also some humorous stories added for your enjoyment and even these are inspired by an actual event or events.

Campfires, Newlyweds, Bigfoot, Rattlesnakes

The flames from the campfire danced and the red coals had that mesmerizing glow that everyone enjoys. I was sitting fireside with my new bride and a few family members. We were having fun camping and of course a campfire is important to laugh and relax around. In fact, I was totally relaxed staring at the coals. I have been fortunate to have many family members be Bigfoot enthusiasts. I think Bigfoot entered each of our minds after what we heard next.

We were in Washington State but near the Canadian border. It is an area that my dad had been going to before I was born. I can't remember how old I was when he first took me there but we would return most every summer for days at a time. It is where I saw my first cougar, bobcat and grizzly bear in the wild. It is where I first heard a cougar scream. This area is where I have been closest to a wild black bear – four feet. Obviously the area is rugged and wild.

I jerked out of my relaxed state, when from the hillside to our south, came a howl. Not just a howl from a smaller animal like a coyote, but it had the volume as if an 800 pound Tarzan bellowed a howl. I looked at everyone around the campfire and they were all staring at or beyond each other. Someone questioned, "What was that – Bigfoot?"

This was before the name Ohio Howl was given to this Bigfoot vocalization. At that time, I had not developed my approach to respond to any possible Bigfoot activity or vocalization. If I knew then what I know now, I would have tried various things to see if more vocalizations would follow.

A couple years later, my oldest nephew and I would have a paralleling experience at the base of the same hill. After hearing a scream, we went down a Forest Service road. Something snapped a stick behind us on our left. We continued to walk. Then a stick would break ahead of us on our left. We continued and this repeated several times. Finally we heard something run behind us and into the brush on our right. We did not get a glimpse of what it was.

When heading home from the camping trip with the howl, we got down to the drier, lower elevations. In the middle of the Forest Service road was a large rattlesnake at least four feet long. I stopped as I neared it. It coiled up in front of the pickup as if to "take on" the truck. My wife and I had been camping in a tent, up to then. My wife said, "Between Bigfoot and rattlesnakes, I'm not sleeping in a tent anymore." The next day we went shopping for an RV.

I have been camping all my life and next I will mention how it all began for me.

Dad

My dad was an avid outdoorsman all his life. I am blessed he passed his love for the outdoors to me and took me hunting and fishing at every chance. He introduced me to how wonderful, and dangerous nature is. He started taking me hunting when I was knee high to a grasshopper (long before I could carry a rifle.) I remember enjoying it, except maybe the part of not being able to catch my breath because I had to take three steps for every one step he took through the woods. But my love for the forest had begun.

When it came to Bigfoot, my dad did not believe. He would say, "I have hunted every mountain in Eastern Washington (which was not much of an exaggeration) and I have never seen one." That did not squelch my passion – see the chapter on passion versus obsession. Each time we were out, I would not say anything, but I was hoping to see tracks and/or a Bigfoot.

My dad was of the belief that when you did something, you worked hard and did it right the first time. He was particular about things and this carried over to campfire wood. Of course the campfire ring had to be in a safe place and well-constructed. It could not be too small, because according to my dad, the length of the firewood had to be about three feet long. You could burn these through the middle, then have the ends to place in the coals. The diameter did not matter but the length did. For example, a dead tree stump about three feet high was just right. But, it could have a root diameter of six feet. I remember the burning of one. I remember seeing the side of his old truck the next morning. It could have been rust areas under the paint or spots where the paint blistered from the extreme heat of the nearby campfire.

Thanks for the memories, Dad.

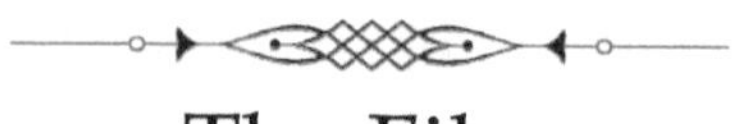

The Film

I was ten years old, living in Spokane County, Washington and heard that Roger Patterson was presenting the famous film at the Spokane Coliseum. My oldest sister and her husband took my oldest nephew and me. I remember Roger standing on stage. When the film started, I still remember what went through my mind. "Look at that animal! Look how it moves! That is not a person in a suit, that is an animal!"

I got Roger's autograph that night and kept it all these years. It is a tiny, but significant part of Bigfoot history. Later, for a membership fee of six dollars, I became a member of his Northwest Research Association. I received his bulletins (newsletters), about three every year. I saved these along with my membership certificate, which are also rare history. I have recently donated his autograph and the original bulletins to the North American Bigfoot Center in Boring, Oregon where they can be seen.

I was hooked and would follow the topic of Bigfoot all through my life. I kept my ears open about any sightings. Back then, there was not social media to post sightings so information came through the "grapevine." I made mental notes about locations. Whenever I was camping or hunting, I kept my eyes and ears open.

I have been very fortunate to have a passion for Bigfoot. I have had many experiences that I can only attribute to Bigfoot, after ruling out other things. When I read a report or interview someone, I want to learn about Bigfoot behavior during that encounter. Most important, are the friends I have made due to this passion.

I have a PowerPoint presentation that I give at expeditions and conferences. It includes quotes from Roger's bulletins. His thoughts and plans were ahead of his time, in my opinion. There are many great thoughts in these bulletins but I will quote my favorites here.

Bulletin No. 3

"Once the expedition is in full swing, the association's Board of Directors will determine helicopter availability, truck transportation, veterinarians and finally alerting the holding area.

....The main camp headquarters will be equipped with hand-held receiver and transmitter units. Also at main camp will be tranquilizing equipment. These groups also experiment with sounding techniques and food type experiments. These are used to try and lure the creatures in. During the day the crews will cover their own area checking all streams, lakes or marshy areas for tracks. They will also be looking for caves or caverns where a creature of this type may hold up. Also, during the day bait lines will be set where tracks can be easily viewed.

Sounding devices will also be rigged for night use. At night, stands will be made. During this time experimental sounds can be tried along with just waiting and watching."

Bulletin No. 4

"We believe these creatures to be extremely intelligent in the ways of the wild. If one is captured it will probably be proven as the most intelligent animal, next to man.
Because of this intelligence, the association believes these creatures can completely
elude man if they so desire."

Passion Or Obsession
The Fine Line

After seeing the Patterson-Gimlin film, I was on my way with a decades-long passion. I began cutting out articles from my local newspaper which often had an article about Bigfoot. My ears were open for anyone saying they heard about a sighting. I would ask about the details and location, even though this information may have come a long way down the "grapevine." I was always on the lookout for anything that could be Bigfoot.

There is a fine line where passion can become obsession. Obsession is when you have lost control and it is all you can think of. I have not reached that point, even though I have had so many encounters, a sighting and I want more. I have heard the term harmonious passion. This is when you partake in something with enjoyment for the activity alone and not for secondary gains. This is the passion I want to continue. I don't need to be in the limelight or make money from the mystery of Bigfoot.

It has been fun to meet television personalities, authors, certified trackers, Bigfoot enthusiasts and other investigators from around North America. I have met Mr. Gimlin multiple times over the years. He is my hero.

It is the mystery I love. Chris Van Allsburg author of "Jumanji" and "The Polar Express" said, "The inclination to believe in the fantastic may strike some as a failure in logic – or gullibility, but it's really a gift. A world that might have Bigfoot and the Loch Ness Monster, is, clearly superior to one that definitely does not."

Have fun out there. Be safe. Remember to press the record button to get video so we can see movement.

Expeditions

When I signed up for my first expedition with the Bigfoot Field Researchers Organization (BFRO), I wondered what it would be like. The people were amazing. My mind was a sponge as I listened to eyewitnesses tell about their encounters and talk about Bigfoot behavior. I understood there was no guarantee of an encounter but I learned so much. Most important was the making of new friends. I knew I needed to attend more. Little did I know that a few years later I would be co-leading expeditions with some great friends.

I consider the encounter that I did have on that first expedition more rare than a sighting.

While scouting one July afternoon, a few of us came to a bench with a tiny stream below and wildlife trails going down to the water. We were looking north to a hillside across from us. The hillside had been logged in the past, but I don't know how many years previous. We could see a basin to our west with the stream running out of it. We had one of those feelings that this would be a great place for a night watch using the lay of the land to our advantage.

Well before dark, I left camp with a husband and wife. We wanted to be in place before dark and quietly sat down in the small bushes on the bench facing the hillside to our north. We arrived a little after 9:00 pm. Shortly after, we heard a couple small rocks rolling at our 12 o' clock. The events that happened next will be listed here as is written in my Bigfoot journal - immediately after the encounter.

*9:33 pm at our 11 o'clock a deer coming from the basin started "blowing." Over the next 10 minutes the deer moved east to our 1 o' clock then acted confused and began circling and going up and down, back and forth in maybe a half acre area on the hillside, blowing the entire time.

*The temperature was dropping and it became very dark. The moon was not yet up.

*10:06 the husband asked me to do a howl as he could not do a good one. I did a loud, long howl toward the basin and ending to our 12 o' clock.

*My ears were ringing from the howl but the husband immediately heard low on the hill and to our right, heavy crashing and thumping, followed by a "yip." He said it sounded like a bulldozer going through the brush.

*I did 2 whoops in that direction, paused, 2 more whoops.

*The deer seemed totally confused – moving back and forth. Then it started moving northeast over the ridge at our 2 o' clock.

*The wife did 2 wood knocks, paused, 1 more.

*Repeated same sequence of knocks.

*Deer came back toward us to the area where it first was circling.

*I did 3 to 4 whoops.

*The husband saw a small light on the hillside at our 11 o' clock.

*I did another long howl.

*Chatter/gibberish was heard from the area of the small light. The chatter was short in length and fairly high pitched, as a young lady talking fast.

*Repeat of chatter at same location.

*The wife did 2 wood knocks.

*Chatter now at our 12 o' clock.

*The wife did 2 more wood knocks.

*The deer, still blowing, made its way toward the location where the chatter was first heard, but went uphill and over the ridge.

*We heard 2 dull wood knocks at our 12 o' clock.

*I did another howl.

*The husband heard crunching/walking on our side of the stream below us (on a game trail?)

*The wife caught a glimpse of a dark shadow to the right.

*We decided to leave. It was 10:30.

We followed the movement of the deer because of its constant blowing. I have never heard a deer be so confused, stay in one spot for so long blowing, and I have hunted deer all my life. It was as if it was corralled in an area for a while. I was in awe when it came back toward the hillside. In fact, an investigator I met on this expedition, said three years later, "The look on your face when you arrived back at camp!"

Our theory was that there may have been four Bigfoot involved in a deer hunting drive. Two pushing it out of the basin. The one the husband heard leave like a bulldozer after my first howl. One that turned the deer back toward the hillside. I will always call this "The Interrupted Sasquatch Deer Hunt" as we seemed to have interrupted their planned hunt.

The next morning, we scoured the hillside. Directly across, at approximately 125 yards from our observation point, two possible Bigfoot tracks were found. First, a 12 ½ inch track was in gritty-sandy-tiny chipped rock soil. It had enough impression to make the track visible, yet we made no indentation in the soil. The ball and big toe of the second track, which was 15 ½ inches, cut into the side of a mound of soil.

I do think it is best to have two or more Bigfoot related activities, different vocalizations, or findings during an encounter to rule out other animals. There were many during this amazing experience.

I immediately began saving for a thermal imager!

As I mentioned, the people I have met on expeditions have been amazing. The fellow BFRO investigators I work closely with are the best. They are volunteers that don't do it for fame or dollars. They are open-minded and have a passion like me. They are my friends. If you have not had a chance to meet them on an expedition or at conferences, you are missing out.

He Does Exist

There was a television commercial where two walking and talking candies see Santa. They say, "He does exist!" Santa says, "They do exist!" One of the candies faint, Santa faints. Seeing is believing? I always ask myself, "What else could it be?" I want to rule out the most common things in the forest. To paraphrase a fellow investigator: almost all of the time it is something else other than Bigfoot, but sometimes, it cannot be anything else but Bigfoot.

May, 2020. It was a sunny day, 2:30 in the afternoon. The two elk were beautiful standing off the Forest Service road as we climbed in elevation. My great friend and fellow investigator was with his wife in their car behind me. Just ahead, I turned on a side road that continued up into the Washington Cascade Mountains toward the snow line. I try to follow the snow line when scouting in the spring because the wildlife is following the melting snow line. Tracks can be readily seen in the mud and patches of snow. This was the case as we saw sign of elk, deer, cougar, bear, and bobcat.

This side road would eventually dead-end. Tree boughs were growing out into the road in places. I came around a corner and I saw up ahead a large boulder on the left edge of the road. It later measured 3 feet 4 inches tall, 3 ½ feet wide and extended up the road 4 ½ feet. A steep open hillside went up to the left. I did notice black between the back of the boulder and the steep hillside but I thought it was just some black decaying wood.

As I approached the boulder, my focus was on how the road was very narrow as it curved around the boulder with a steep drop off to the right. Suddenly, a black figure leaped from behind the boulder and when it landed on the right edge of the road, all I could see was a black butt because of boughs that extended into the road. It paused, then went over the embankment, down the steep hillside on my right. The figure resembled a linebacker, viewed from the side, leaping to sack the quarterback. It was not upright, so I estimate the height and weight similar to a linebacker: 6' 4", 240 pounds. Hair length was similar to a bear but I did not see a round body like a bear. No bear nose or ears were seen. In fact, I did not see any front legs or arms extended out. There was a lot of space between the ground and the chest. I was confused because there appeared to be a wing tip sticking up from the lower back. Your mind goes to things you see the most. After a while, I realized the arms were back along the torso and what I thought was a wing tip, was its fingers sticking up.

With my truck ahead of them and tree boughs sticking into the road, my friend and his wife did not see the figure. We stopped and my friend looked at the right edge of the road and pointed out two impressions where two feet possibly landed. I looked over the embankment and saw a slide track on the hillside. This small area of the hillside was open. Several feet below the slide track was a skid in the hillside leaving just a line of exposed dirt. Trees were present below the skid line. If it had been a bear or moose, there should have been straddle disturbances in the soil from four legs. We went to the track and saw angled toes but also where dirt was pushed up from other toes!

I always try to take pictures of possible tracks from all angles and get down on my knees to look into each track and study it. When I got near the track I slipped and slid on my hip downhill. I did not want to fall into the track and ruin it. I thought, "Forget the pictures and just cast it." As I was pouring the cast material, I watched in panic as it began to run downhill. I wasn't sure I could get a good cast.

The cast turned out well and would be evidence of the sighting. It is that extra evidence one always hopes to get with an encounter. A copy of the cast can be seen at the North American Bigfoot Center as noted in the chapter about Boring, Oregon.

Ten weeks later, we were at this location for an official expedition. A fellow investigator, who I call one of my good luck charms, had to leave one morning. On her way out, on the lower road, she saw a black upright figure enter the tree line ahead and off to the side. She estimated the height to be about 6' 10".

I know everyone is asking one question: why didn't I have a dash camera to record a Bigfoot leap across the road? Well, I have one with the suction cup mount that attaches to the inside of my front windshield. However, the action camera was not working at that time. I have rectified that.

It's Not Boring in Boring

I have thought for a long time that I should donate my Bigfoot history items so they can be seen by all Bigfoot enthusiasts. In 2021 I donated Roger Patterson's autograph, his original bulletins, my original membership certificate from his Northwest Research Association and various articles I had saved. I went to Boring, Oregon and donated this history to Cliff Barackman for his North American Bigfoot Center (NABC). I am so happy that this little bit of history will continue to be seen. At the NABC, Cliff already had on display an original poster advertising Roger Patterson presenting "The Film" at the Portland, Oregon Coliseum and the Spokane, Washington Coliseum. I quote from the poster, "SEE Roger Paterson (The first man yet to film Bigfoot) as he comes face to face with one of these giant creatures!"

I also took the cast from my sighting to show Cliff. He said, "That's a track!" He asked if he could borrow it to make copies. It is a sliding track because it was over the edge of the road on a hillside. We discussed every track is not going to be perfect in mud, etc. A copy of my cast can be seen at the North American Bigfoot Center.

Having Cliff immediately want to make copies of my cast was the icing on the cake of my sighting. I will repeat myself about the importance of having two or more Bigfoot activities, vocalizations, or findings during an encounter to rule out other animals. The more investigating you can do, the more evidence will be found.

The North American Bigfoot Center is fantastic. I highly recommend every Bigfoot enthusiast visit there.

Or, if you are a skeptic, I still highly recommend a visit to see the history and evidence.

The Look on Their Faces

Etched in my mind forever are the looks on various people's faces. Some after an encounter, while others during a conversation about Bigfoot.

One such memory is when my wife heard wood knocks for the first time. The sun was out and the spring temperatures were rising. Such contrast to a couple weeks before when my wife and I tried to explore the same mountain trail and ran into snow and fog. I think there is no better time for exploring than to follow the melting snow line. That day, ours was the only vehicle at the trailhead and we did not see anyone. The trail became steeper. It's like the old joke: "This trail looked flatter on the map!" We had been quietly hiking, enjoying another chance to be in the mountains. We paused to catch our breath, then heard very close and loud: knock – knock, knock, knock! It was wood on wood. I will never forget the look on my wife's face. She knew exactly what it was but said, "I really hope that was a giant woodpecker!" My wife is fine with Bigfoot as long as they are fifty miles away, not fifty feet. I am just the opposite. We had no chance of seeing anything due to the thick brush and trees at this spot. Of course, it was a great spot for a Bigfoot to listen to what was using the trail and remain concealed. People speculate what a wood knock means. I wonder what does the pattern/sequence of knocks mean. I also wonder, can Bigfoot really tell the difference between wood knocks and chopping wood? I have returned to this area many times since. I have never heard so many knocks and whoops from one area over time. My wife would also hear her first whoops in this area during a separate hike. I have had rocks thrown at my camp table and an investigator that is near and dear to me would have a quick sighting. When you find an area with history, keep exploring.

I have been very fortunate to have had many, many Bigfoot encounters over the years or be camping with people that did. Another time in the above mentioned area, I was standing next to another investigator. We had been listening to a coyote howl just out of sight in the trees, very close to camp. It moved to the east and we heard another howl at the end of the coyote howl. Bigfoot, or another coyote? The coyote came back! I was watching a gap in the trees to the northeast and my fellow investigator was watching a gap to the east. He said something like, did you see that - it was black. I asked if it had a horizontal back, like a moose. "It was no moose," he said. There was that look. I'll never forget it. The look on his face told me all I needed to know. I will not go into the details here but upon recreation it was upright, about 7 ½ feet tall. It walked through a small gap and apparently went down a game trail that went east behind a giant fir tree. That is why he did not see it come out the other side of the fir and thus "disappeared" back into the forest.

When you own a small business, you wear many hats and are constantly busy. I was happy when I had an hour for lunch. One day at lunchtime, I went down the street for some quick shopping. They had a small book section and something drew me to it. There was a book about Bigfoot and I clutched it as if it was a piece of gold. A young lady started to scan my items at checkout. She picked up the Bigfoot book and paused. She asked, "Bigfoot, is he really out there?"

I spoke before thinking and blurted out the first thing that popped in my mind, "Yes, I have even heard them talking!"

From the look on her face, I thought she was going to call security. I then realized I was probably at the top of her list of unconventional customer interactions. I hope she didn't quit at the end of her shift, citing the escalating craziness of the customers. I did have to smile. Price of the book, $15. Look on her face, priceless.

The Eyes Have It

As a veterinarian, I am very curious about Bigfoot anatomy. What is the anatomy from their senses, to digestion of various foods that would make you and I sick, to their hands and of course, their feet? One anatomical part where I have great interest, is the eyes. What could their eyes be like? I have a PowerPoint presentation that I have given many times on expeditions. This is my opinion of what their eyes and vision may be like. It is all "what-ifs" because obviously we don't have an eye to biopsy. As a veterinarian, I just have to write a little about anatomy!

Eight reasons why Bigfoot may have excellent day and night vision:

*They have a large eyeball which means the back of eye is very large. Thus, the eye would contain a huge amount of rods. These are the photoreceptor cells that are very sensitive to light and help have vision in low light conditions. So, Bigfoot has a great advantage over us in low light.

*The large eye would have a huge amount of cones. These are the photoreceptor cells that allow us to see color.

*A fovea is a pit or depression in the back of eye with closely packed cones and allows us to see detail. If Bigfoot has a fovea, their day vision is well defined. They can easily see whether a person is carrying an axe or a hunter carrying a rifle.

*Their pupil can open multiple times the diameter of the human pupil. This allows more light to enter.

*The human lens has a yellow filter to remove ultraviolet light. Deer do not have this filter so they see well at night. What if Bigfoot does not have this filter to their lens?

*What if Bigfoot has the reflective layer (Tapetum Lucidum) to the back of the eye like dogs, cats, bear, elk and deer? This layer reflects light back onto the rods increasing the light available to the rods and increasing night vision.

*What if Bigfoot has an extra cone that is not sensitive to color but to UV light? This would increase night vision further.

*What if Bigfoot can see infrared light? Many people think they can see the infrared from trail cameras.

A closing thought about eye shine versus eye glow in the Bigfoot eye. I like to separate the two. It is just me, but I call eye shine the reflected light from the back of the eye. There needs to be a light source such as a flashlight or bright moonlight shining into the eye. Eye glow, to me, means light production such as bioluminescence, which is light produced by living cells and seen in total darkness. This is a discussion for another time.

My Bigfoot Girlfriend

Oh, the fun memories! I want to enjoy the outdoors with family and friends. Of course, there is always kidding each other about the actions of people and Bigfoot. I repeat myself, that one objective is to make Bigfoot feel comfortable enough to come into camp. If I have to be their entertainment, so be it. Careful what you wish for, is the saying, as they may not only be in camp but are they trying to enter my tent also?

First, I want to mention the throwing of objects by Bigfoot especially at tents and the accuracy they seem to have. Once, my tent was set up on a gravel area so I placed a vinyl tarp under it. That tent was not tall enough to stand in and I had to bend over or get on my knees to open the door. So I left about fourteen inches of tarp out from the door to kneel on while entering. I did not hear anything walking, but I was awakened at dawn by the sound of something hitting near my tent. My first thought was a squirrel in the tree behind me dropped something down onto my tent. But, then there was another sound and I realized it was apparently a small rock that hit the strip of tarp in front of the door. I listened to about a dozen rocks hit in almost the same place. When I did open the door, I saw these little rocks. I realized later the accuracy of the thrower. Not one rock bounced off the tent. I don't think a person could be that accurate. If Bigfoot has such accuracy, I believe it is easy for them to hit a grouse, wild turkey or any animal that looks good for lunch.

There have been many times when I heard bipedal walking around my tent. I have been laying with my face near the tent wall and could hear the step land just on the other side of the wall, inches from my face. There have been many times I've heard stomping outside my tent and instead of finding deer tracks the next morning, foot impressions are seen in the angle of the morning sun. Other times, casts have been made of tracks found behind tents.

My tent has been shaken violently many times after hearing bipedal walking. It was not a bear pushing its nose into the wall. But, the tent was shaking to the point I wondered if the tent stakes would come out of the ground. I use tent nails, not the small, easily bent stakes. I have thought, "What is it doing? Is it trying to come in?" I believe they know a person is coming out when they hear the sound of a tent or sleeping bag zipper. They would run and be into the trees before I could get out of my sleeping bag and tent with a thermal imager. Therefore, I let them feel comfortable about being in camp and maybe return the next night. Another point is that I want to learn from what they are doing – what is attracting them. I let them do what they are going to do. Also, I want the other people in camp to have an experience. Finally, what if I am mistaken and it is a black bear or grizzly bear outside my tent? It would not be safe to jump out and be face to face.

The numerous times of something trying to get into my tent started some kidding by a couple fellow investigators who I like to call my good luck charms. We have had many shared experiences, not to mention the fun we have when we get together! They have morphed the story into my having a Bigfoot girlfriend trying to get into my tent. All my work to attract Bigfoot has resulted in one having a crush on me (everything is big with Bigfoot, so it is a huge crush!) They go on to warn me that tonight, my girlfriend will bring her kids. Or, her "husband" may show up.

I let them go on and on. "As long as she doesn't stink," I reply.

Vocalizations

The four most spoken words by Bigfoot enthusiasts that spend time in the woods are, "Did you hear that?" Whether you are deep in the woods listening for a Bigfoot vocalization or enjoying the company of friends around a campfire, those four words will be said. I guarantee it.

The silence of the dark woods can be peaceful. When that silence is broken, it can be eerie if my mind allows. That tiny twig snap can start out in my mind as, "That's a field mouse." But then it grows, "That is a wood rat. No, it sounds like it weighs thirty pounds with teeth. Could be one hundred pounds with teeth and claws. I think it is 300 pounds with teeth and claws. It must be Bigfoot!" Runaway thoughts must not be allowed.

I listen for various Bigfoot vocalizations when no other people are around. But what if some vocalizations are actually from another stinky creature that has been in the woods for a bit – humans?

For example, maybe a husband and wife set up camp far down the road while I was out all day scouting and starting audio recorders. I don't know they are camped back in the trees. I may think the following are vocalizations from Bigfoot but I would be mistaken.

Gibberish: It is actually the husband's long rant of swear words after he runs into a stump with their truck.

Whistle: It is actually the wife looking at the damage!

Whoop: The wife after she set up a tent for the first time in her life and it is standing even with two poles not used.

Howl: It is actually the husband's response after he slams his fingers in the truck door.

Scream: It is actually the wife's response when she learns the husband only brought chili and beer.

High pitched gibberish: The wife's rant, that due to obnoxious fumes, he will not be sleeping in the tent with her after his consumption of chili and beer. He must sleep in the truck.

Knock: The truck door slamming!

There have been times, after sitting on a log too long, my back tightens up. I have emitted a sound that would raise the hair on a grizzly and send it running. The pain in my lower back results in a scream that carries for miles. I walk hunched, looking like a Bigfoot. I wonder if that is why I have a Bigfoot girlfriend?

35

Men of the Mountains

After spending a lot of time in the mountains of Montana, North Idaho, Washington and Oregon, one must guard against becoming too confident about surviving nature. A person can begin to think they are a mountain man.

We were on a trail – location top secret. My fellow investigator checked his Hikers' Watch and said, "We've hiked 4.2 miles and gained 4,000 feet in elevation."

"My feet and back hurt," I groaned, wiping the sweat from my head. "We haven't seen any track that could be close to Bigfoot. The view is worth it, however!"

"Let's go around the next corner, then turn back. We will heat up the propane barbeque when we get back to camp!"

"Sounds great," I said. The vision of meat cooking on the barbeque made me forget about my feet and back.

After rounding the corner, we were surprised at what we saw below. There stood a tiny shack that had seen better days, with a stove pipe sticking out of the roof. Next to the shack was a small motorhome. I would bet it was made in the 1960s because of the faded orange and green stripes on the sides. Beyond the shanty and motorhome was an outhouse.

A huge t-shirt, yellowed with age or whatever, was covering a window of the shack. The shirt moved and we both dove on the ground expecting a rifle barrel to come out the window.

"Let's go down there and ask if they have had any Bigfoot activity," I said.

"Are you nuts?"

My excitement was now building. "There could be a real mountain man down there that has befriended Bigfoot! We can't let this chance to interview him slip by!"

"I don't want to end up in a book about people gone missing in the woods!" my friend replied. "Besides, I think there is a Bigfoot nearby – do you smell that odor?"

"We are downwind from the outhouse – and the shack – and the motorhome," I answered.

As we were walking toward the shack, I thought I heard a banjo, but my mind went into denial. We walked around to the front of the hovel and saw a tree that had deer, elk and moose antlers nailed to it. Some were white from years of weather exposure but some were new. Some were placed in the branches at an unbelievable height. The number of antlers would rival the number of shoes on a shoe tree. If you have never seen a shoe tree in the woods, it is a sight to behold – for about ten seconds.

"Hello, anyone in there?" I shouted as we approached.

I'm sure you can imagine what emerged from the shack without many details. Actually, I only remember a few details. Because he was taller than the door, he had to duck so as not to knock off his skunk fur hat. He held a muzzleloader rifle. I want to say his skin was like leather but his face was covered with a beard a yard long. From inside the beard, a small bird flew away.

"We are hiking in the National Forest," I said.

"I live on da edge of it," he replied.

"How long have you lived here? Have you ever seen or heard anything out of the ordinary?" I did not mention Bigfoot at first so as not to risk him thinking we were crazed Bigfoot believers.

"Once saw a mountain lion with fangs ten inches long!"

I wondered if he had been there in the time of saber-toothed tigers. "Hmmm, anything else?" I prodded. "I have heard about Bigfoot in these mountains."

"Bigfoot? You believe they exist?"

By his mannerisms, I thought he was hiding something. "Well, I have a passing interest in the subject," I said. "We should be on our way." I thought about asking if we could camp on his property but then I heard banjo music again.

On our way back, my friend said, "That was an experience, but a zero for Bigfoot activity."

"No way! Didn't you see those Bigfoot tracks under that tree? That's how those antlers were placed in the high branches! He's a man of the mountains, like us, and is friends with Bigfoot! They gift him antlers! I grabbed some hair hanging on a lower antler but I don't know if it is from Bigfoot or his beard...... What did you bring for the barbeque?"

The Lake

The Pacific Northwest is filled with many lakes. Maybe not as many as other parts of the United States but there is an abundant amount for fishing, boating, canoeing, swimming and all other water activities. The residents go often. However, when asked what someone did over the weekend, the usual reply is, "We went to the lake!" For some reason, they don't say a lake name. It's as if they expect you to know the exact lake, or since there are so many, they don't think you care which one.

There is one lake for me which does not evoke relaxation. It creeps me out every time I have gone there to camp and/or fish. This is the only location where I have had such a feeling over the years. The location of this mountain lake shall remain top secret because I am sure Bigfoot are nearby.

Creepy things have happened to me there over the years. This can allow my mind to jump to conclusions. Such as when I hear a one pound squirrel in the dark trees at dusk and I think it is a 1,000 pound Bigfoot. One time, near the opposite shore, I was standing in my float tube in hip deep water and casting for fish. A beaver head popped up just in front of me. I could see the evil in its eyes as it stared at me. It was probably just a curious beaver but its stare creeped me out. I convinced myself it had rabies and at any moment, would shred my float tube on its way to my legs. It was closer than the length of my fishing rod. I wondered if the rod would be strong enough to push it away. My float tube and legs were undamaged.

I am sure Bigfoot watches this lake and that was confirmed in my mind one night. Several of us had been sitting on the edge of the lake for hours scanning with our thermal imagers. I tried some things to pique their curiosity but it remained very quiet. I scanned one last time with my thermal. We decided to call it quits and started up the trail behind us. We stopped in our tracks as there was a crashing branch break followed by three wood knocks down the shoreline. I wanted to yell out, "How long have you been watching us?"

When another investigator asks me if I know a spooky lake to camp near, I reply, "I know just the one!" I don't mention my beaver phobia.

The Ultimate Bigfooting Vehicle

I dream about having the ultimate Bigfooting vehicle. It would need to have tires the size of a garage door and be able to scale a cliff to get to a cave where Bigfoot is living. It also would cross any river. Not likely to be needed, it would be equipped with life preservers, inflatable raft and oars.

The exterior and interior must be camouflaged to match the forest. It would have red headlights. This would confuse Bigfoot as to what was coming up the road and he would stand in the road, waiting. I would say, "Gotcha on camera!"

The vehicle would have action cameras inside every window except the side doors. No need for side doors because all passengers should be able to jump out immediately with their thermal imagers and parabolic microphones. Can't waste time opening a door. There also would be thermal imagers all over the roof pointing in every direction, even up into the trees. There would be a thermal imager under the vehicle because you never know if momma Bigfoot hid baby Bigfoot in a pothole.

It would have the most up-to-date GPS. I still want a guarantee that the GPS will not tell me to turn where I end up one thousand feet lower in elevation and have to scale a cliff back up.

Mounted across the hood of the vehicle would be several tranquilizer guns that are fired by motion sensors. This would fire a volley of tranquilizer darts at a Bigfoot crossing the road. The odds favor tranquilizing a deer, so there must be a barbeque in the back of the vehicle for cooking venison.

Most of the rear of the vehicle is taken up by the cage. Yes, a cage is needed for transporting the tranquilized Bigfoot. On the little trailer that is being towed behind the vehicle is a forklift. How else am I going to get the Bigfoot in the cage?

In reality, I don't have anything like that. I usually try to go where few people have gone before but last year I blew or damaged three tires. One sidewall looked like it needed emergency hernia surgery, which being a veterinarian, I could have done. My wife said I should just get another new and better tire. Also, I am happy when my truck gets fifteen miles to the gallon – that's for both gas and oil.

Equipment

After decades in pursuit of this mystery, to say I have collected a lot of equipment for camping and Bigfooting would be an understatement. Take trail cameras. I must "hide" one on top of every truck tire. A couple on the truck bumper. One tied to the truck grill. Many around my tent. Many around camp. Several on each game trail within a mile radius.

Audio recorders also need to be placed with almost every trail camera and one inside my tent. Also, several around the nearby lake.

My first aid kit has become a tote bin all its own. From sutures, to surgical instruments, to stop bleeding powder, tourniquets, slings, splints, elastic wraps, on and on. Because you never know. There is always that one person who has a chainsaw and multiple axes, besides me. There is one investigator that still wears his open toed boots on warm days. I won't go into details, but he did not remove the front of the boots on purpose.

My wife wonders why I have so many tote bins.

"Extra pillows," I answered. "If my tent leaks in the rain, my pillow could get wet." I don't think she believes that because once, I forgot my pillow and she asked why I was holding my head and neck awkward when I got home. I made the mistake of mentioning I forgot my pillow and slept on a rolled up sweatshirt.

Then she points to the bin that contains one hundred pounds of batteries to operate all the equipment and asks "Why is that one so heavy?"

"Extra Blankets. If my tent leaks, my blanket could get wet."

Then there is everything to carry when leaving camp in the evening to be in the woods at night. It takes an hour to get ready. Headlamp, plus four action cameras on my head pointed to the front, rear and each side. Thermal imager. Audio recorder. Extra batteries. First aid items. Rain gear. Some survival items including snacks, water, etc. In fact, after I have everything on, I cannot walk due to the weight. Bigfoot likes to come into camp and snoop around. Maybe I'll just sit in my chair.

Technology

They say technology advances faster and faster. Too fast for me. I'm sure I have cranked a vehicle window more in my lifetime than pushed a button. Of course, technology has entered into all aspects of Bigfooting. It is good to have satellite texting for safety purposes. It is good to be able to see into the darkness for safety and hopefully see a Bigfoot. And on and on. But I grew up using good ol' woodsmanship skills.

I was driving one evening and two of my fellow investigators were using geo maps on their smart phones. We were miles back in the Washington Cascade Mountains. If I had a dollar for every side road and trail we passed, I could buy a drone. My navigators were talking back and forth about what they were seeing on their apps. I was grinning because I would hear "We are heading west."

I would think, "No duh, the sun sets in the west, always has!"

We came to a fork in the road and had to stop. My two companions were outside the truck discussing how far to Mineral Springs and how far to Flat Top Mountain. I had walked across the road to answer the call of nature. I looked up at a faded Forest Service sign, barely readable, with a tree bough hanging in front of it. I announced it was 2.8 miles to Mineral Springs down this road and 1.6 miles to Flat Top Mountain on the road to the left. They looked up from their phones and the look on their faces was astonishment about how I knew exact mileage. They stared at me as if I was an alien with thorough knowledge of the planet. I thought it was hilarious. As I climbed back in the truck, I grinned and said, "Which way do you want to go first?"

Bigfoot Items

Maybe some of you collected marbles when young or at some point in your life. All the names for the various types! I wanted to collect many of each type as a youngster. After decades of interest in Bigfoot, I have collected so many Bigfoot items they may number more than the number of marbles in a large bag. Clothing, caps, mugs, tumblers, picture frames, items such as keychains and refrigerator magnets….on and on.

Of course, many of these Bigfoot items must be taken along camping. The following has not happened yet, but could after I arrive in camp….

"That's a cool looking Bigfoot t-shirt," my fellow investigator said, eyeing my swag. "I think it would fit me."

"I just got it," I proudly reply.

"What else did you bring?"

"Of course I have a Bigfoot mug and tumbler, several magnets in my truck" I answer. Then I get my clothes bag and several caps out of my truck.

"I'll trade you this sweatshirt of Bigfoot carrying a Christmas tree for that t-shirt," he said.

The parlay was on. Things were getting serious and I act as if I am in serious thought.

"I'll take your sweatshirt with Bigfoot wearing sunglasses plus your mug and that cap for this cool looking t-shirt," I said.

"Rather than the Bigfoot wearing sunglasses, I'll give you….wait, what is that t-shirt in your bag?"

"This one?" I ask. "I'm also a Trekkie!" Now we are bolding going into a whole new world of trading!!!

Can't Find a Snowflake in a Snowstorm

I quote Roger Patterson as he wrote in his Northwest Research Association bulletins: Bulletin No. 2

"Most occurrences have happened as complete surprises. The creatures seem to come all of a sudden, then leave as if they were never there."

My sighting was just that – happened as a complete surprise. I believe they can hide and allow us to pass by. I believe they know when to remain motionless. I believe they blend in to the terrain – hide in plain sight. Bigfoot is the hide and seek champion. I previously quoted from Roger Patterson's bulletins, "These creatures can completely elude man if they so desire."

Sometimes I feel trying to spot a Bigfoot is the same as: I can't find a snowflake in a snowstorm. They can be close and yet remain unseen. For example, more than once, I've had wood knocks so close, I about jumped out of my camping chair. Yet they were not seen, even with thermal imaging.

Sometimes, it seems Bigfoot is everywhere. It has become big business. Merchandise of all types from clothing to decals to statues. Many people have named their business Bigfoot such and such. For example, if I was an electrician, "Kevin's Bigfoot Electric – We don't want you to get zapped!" Okay, I'm not discussing the real thing, now.

You may be a skeptic, but there is something out there. There are too many sightings for all of us to be wrong. So, embrace the mystery, but question everything. Spend time in the woods and like Bigfoot, leave no trace.

A Letter to Bigfoot, From Kevin's Wife

Dear Bigfoot,

I am writing this to let you know all the inconveniences you have caused over the years. I am not happy with the amount of time Kevin spends looking for you.

There are the number of hours Kevin spends reading reports about your teasing of other people.

There are the times he has gone to conferences and Bigfoot festivals and left me home. Although, I really don't need to listen to other people because I am constantly listening to my own "speaker" (Kevin) all year long.

I can't begin to count the days that Kevin has been gone on "camping" trips. I loosely refer to them as camping trips because they are really scouting trips. Scouting for you. I don't need to attend these because I don't want you around. I am jealous of you stealing Kevin away. Plus, I have to listen to Kevin for hours upon his return about your antics around and in camp.

There is also the time spent planning and going on expeditions. I am also given detailed reports about your behavior on these.

When Kevin returns from all these trips, he is exhausted. You keep him up at night with your shenanigans, whistles, knocks, whoops, etc. You move things in camp, play with camp stoves, stomp around camp and shake tents. Kevin also is beat up with scratches and scrapes from crawling over dead downed trees looking for your tracks that you only occasionally leave, just to tease. Kevin has mosquito bites, bee stings and tick bites. Long ago, I should have bought stock in companies making bandages, sting relief spray products and triple antibiotic ointment.

His truck is a sight to see when he returns. I don't know who is more banged up, Kevin or the truck? There is enough dust in the back of the truck to build another mile of mountain road and enough pine needles to stuff a mattress.

The amount of camping equipment in our basement is impressive but overwhelming. Every time we are in a sporting goods store, he remarks he should buy another or new item for camping. How many cots does one person need? You can only sleep on one at a time.

Also, how many different cameras and audio recorders does a person need?

Then there is the money spent on a drone that is now in the top of a very tall tree. Kevin said something about a wind gust. He also mumbled something about he was recording you chasing some elk and was focused on that, not the trees. I hope you are happy. I don't know how you do it but you avoided being filmed one more time because the recording of you chasing elk is in the top of a tree in Montana. Apparently, the big skies of Montana are not big enough for Kevin to fly a drone.

I asked Kevin to give you this letter, but he looked at me like I was from a different planet. So, I am putting this letter in his tent bag hoping it falls on the ground for you when he takes his tent out. (But, which tent is he taking?)

If you would just be quiet, stop your mischief and stay in a cave somewhere. Kevin will never find you there due to his claustrophobia.

Signed,
Kevin's wife.

P.S. Not to mention his dream of the ultimate bigfooting vehicle, which he constantly talks about in his sleep.

Incessantly Bigfooting

I like the word investigator rather than researcher because investigating implies more detective work. I feel I have been very fortunate with many encounters over the decades. When I hear something and/or have an encounter, I always question, "What else could it be other than Bigfoot?" This is the first thing that runs through my mind. I need to rule out the most common things in the forest first. To paraphrase one of my fellow investigators: almost all of the time it is something else other than Bigfoot, but sometimes, it cannot be anything else but Bigfoot. As I mentioned previously, I hope to have two or more Bigfoot related activities, different vocalizations, or findings occur during an encounter. This tilts the scale in favor of Bigfoot in my opinion.

It is important for me to have fun and enjoy friends, fellow enthusiasts, and all the forests and mountains have to offer. Every investigator has their own approach (whatever works for you) but I have many things I do to hopefully increase the chances of an encounter. If I have to be their entertainment, so be it. I feel I have been very successful doing this. I may try playing a musical instrument. I'm not a musician but Bigfoot doesn't know that. When possible Bigfoot activity begins, then it is time to be serious. I want the encounter to continue.

I go into the mountains with an attitude of respect for the forest and Bigfoot. I feel I am just a visitor to their home. I have never had a feeling of dread (that's not to say my heart rate has never been at the maximum - for example, the times when my tent was shaking and I thought my tent stakes were going to lift out of the ground.) I don't know if that is due to my attitude that I always try to project. I want Bigfoot to do whatever they want and I want them to feel comfortable to return to my camp night after night.

I will continue trying to increase my chances of an encounter. I will continue to investigate this mystery. Every sighting and encounter is a piece of the puzzle. I will continue with harmonious passion – not needing secondary gains such as fame or dollars. I will be out there looking for tracks, hoping to hear two or more different Bigfoot vocalizations, or see another

one. If not, that's fine. But I will be incessantly
Bigfooting.

About the Author

Kevin Llewellyn grew up in eastern Washington State and currently lives in Spokane, Washington with his wife, Carol. He graduated from Washington State University College of Veterinary Medicine. Now retired, he was a veterinarian for thirty five years, owning his own practice for twenty eight years.

He has camped, fished and hunted all his life.

At ten years old, he saw Roger Patterson in person present the Patterson-Gimlin film at the Spokane Coliseum in Spokane, Washington. He was immediately hooked and has been following the topic of Bigfoot since. Kevin got Roger Patterson's autograph that night not knowing it would be a tiny but significant piece of history in the timeline of the Bigfoot topic. Kevin also became a member of Roger's Northwest Research Association and received bulletins/newsletters. Kevin put those aside with many other articles about Bigfoot and years later they are also a rare part of Bigfoot history. These can be seen at the North American Bigfoot Center in Boring, Oregon.

Through all the years, every time Kevin is in the woods, he has kept open the possibility of Bigfoot activity occurring. He has had many and varied encounters over his decades of following the Bigfoot topic.